I0445499

SKILLFUL MOANERS

VERY WILD THINGS

TENA SELDAN

plicit Press

CHAPTER 1

"NERVOUS?" Ashley asked Jillian as they stood side by side in front of the full-length mirror in Ashley's bedroom.

"Not at all. I just wish we weren't going after one position. Would've been cool to work together!"

"Maybe not," Ashley said, a silly smile on her face. "You know how we are when we're together."

"I know," Jillian replied. "Might have been fun is all I'm saying!"

The pair of striking beauties had been roommates at Penn State, where they both worked toward and achieved Marketing Degrees. The school was easy, both of them that combination of brains and looks that most men, and women, found intimidating. So the coursework was easy for them. So easy, actually, that they often found themselves doing crazy things, just to beat the boredom.

They also both just like doing crazy things!

Ashley was exotically beautiful, an Asian/Latin mix. Jillian was more classical in her beauty and fiery red hair thanks to her Irish immigrant genes. Their looks might have been different. Their appetite for *naughty* was not.

Feeding off each other came naturally to them. They were perfectly in tune with each other, much to their benefit, and to the pleasure of anyone they happened to have in their sights.

There was that one time, in their second semester, for example, where another marketing student, James Royden, attempted to date both of them, unaware that the two had already become firm friends. This was college, they both knew, but the pair would not be played, not even by the hottest guy on campus.

James hadn't slept with either of them, yet, but he felt that he was close. Both young women knew that he wanted to seal the deal soon, and so, over hot chocolate and Oreo's, they came up with a deliciously wicked plan for payback.

Ashley would lure James to a downtown motel. She played on James's ego, although this was unnecessary because he really needed little convincing to take the opportunity to display his abilities, mastered in the first six months of college, really. He didn't mind not having to *work* for Ashley, who seemed suddenly more *willing* than Jillian.

Jillian was in no way playing hard to get, of course. She really liked James but didn't like being outwitted by someone who really wasn't as smart as he thought. Yes, she and Ashley were not close yet, and sat at opposite ends of the lecture halls, mostly, but given that all three of them attended the same lectures, it really was shortsighted of James to assume that he could have them both without them finding out.

So Jillian took to her part in this revenge plot quite seriously. She was assigned to get a random hottie from campus to the same motel room, seduce him, and make sure that James was witness to this.

The plan was actually a little more meticulous, more

erotically evil than this, though. And it played out perfectly. Almost too perfectly, in fact.

The *random college hottie* wasn't a stranger at all, not to the three college students. He was the janitor who would come in and out of their lecture halls emptying bins. And it was no accident that Jillian chose him.

Ty was tall and a little too skinny. He had a mischievous almost gangster vibe about him and usually spoke to no one, probably because he was in his late 20s and could have if life was fair, been a student at the University he worked at as a cleaner. African American, he spoke like he was from the *ghetto* when he did speak of course, and so, of all the possibilities, he was the one who would piss the egotistical James off the most!

Jillian got to the motel first, having told Ty their plan, Ty was more than willing to go along with it. He had absolutely no problem being *used* by the beautiful college co-eds he knew he would otherwise never have had the opportunity to be with. He wouldn't have done it, of course, had he known James personally, or if James had spoken to him with respect, or even if James just wasn't so much of a *douchebag*.

Mr. Royden walked around campus like his father owned the place. And Ty was excited about bringing him off his high horse, almost as excited as he was at the thought of what he was about to do with Jillian, and Ashley if he'd understood the plot correctly.

They went to the bathroom and closed the door. Jillian pulled Ty down to her and kissed him long on his mouth, his lips full and soft. Ty pressed himself against her, pushing her against the door. She could feel that he was already locked and loaded, hard and ready for his performance.

He wouldn't have to wait too long, too, because they

soon heard the door open. They remained quiet as Ashley got her part done. She sat James on a chair after getting him completely naked and tied him to the chair with cuffs she had brought for just this purpose. James was incredibly excited, already dripping from his solid shaft, thick and long between his thighs.

Ashley excused herself, said she'd be right back, and slipped into the bathroom. When she exited, she was completely naked, her hair out of her bun, hanging beautifully down her back and shoulders. She got onto the bed and teased herself with two additional pairs of handcuffs. James looked at her, a little confused, but he felt that she could do whatever she wanted, given the promise of the situation.

Then Jillian exited the bathroom, also naked, her fiery locks falling like a river down her back. She didn't even look at James as she got on the bed with Ashley, the two women touching themselves and each other.

James looked like he'd just been caught out, with his pants down. He had, and his pants lay in a heap on the floor in front of him. He smiled his best smile, insisting that this night could still be fun, for all three of them. He tried his best to convince the two vixens, pleading with them now, his meat throbbing where it was still rock hard. The combination of the two stunners in front of him sent him into almost *primal beast mode*!

Just then, a tall, skinny African American with *nine* solid inches dangling in front of him exited the bathroom.

"Sup?" Ty said to James, winking, before he got between Ashley and Jillian and let them cuff him to the bed...

CHAPTER 2

"WE REALLY DID SOME CRAZY THINGS," Jillian said as Ashley held the door to *Wild Things* open for her. They were about an hour early for their interview, but they didn't mind. Both of them wanted to absorb the feel of the boutique advertising agency in the hope that this would give them an added advantage.

The waiting room was nice. It was trendy and colorful but not *too much*. The large red reception desk was obviously designed for the space, and as the two women sat opposite it, they caught their reflection in the red.

"We look good," Ashley said, speaking of herself mostly.

"We do," said Jillian as she pulled her skirt down just a bit. Every man that passed them in the waiting room looked at their legs before they looked at their faces, and Jillian, slightly more conservative, *just slightly*, felt a little under-dressed. Although, there was no shortage of provocative outfits in the building.

"Oh stop it. This place thrives on sex and lust. Apparently, the executives believe it fuels creativity!"

Jillian looked at Ashley quizzically, not sure if she was serious. "Where did you hear that?"

"You didn't read the link I sent you, did you?"

"I did!" Jillian lied.

Ashley knew that she was lying, though, because if she had, she would have known that in a recent interview, Charles van der Haus, founder and head creative of Wild Things, said just that.

'I find, especially with young people, that where you eliminate modern restrictions and allow them to act out sexually at work, this frees up their energy for creativity. It boosts creativity in fact. And for older men like me, this access to sex without restrictions or taboo, without stuffy rules and protocols, keeps us young, and reminds us of who we are!'

These were his exact words.

"Miss Jones, they're ready for you!"

Ashley and Jillian got up together, Jillian making sure that nothing on her friend was out of place. Then she wished her luck and watched as she disappeared into the double doors leading to the conference room.

"Miss Jones, this is Rod and Ben. And I'm Charles." He stood up as she got to the table, and shook her hand as the other two men stood up. Charles wore a pair of distressed denim jeans and a vest, and Rod and Ben wore chinos and golf shirts.

Ashley guessed correctly that everyone who was actually *dressed for the office* here must have been new, and not yet acclimatized to the casual culture.

"Please, call me Ashley!" she said, sitting down in the seat closest to them. She pushed her seat out just enough for the three men to get a better view of her legs. Ashley wasn't against the use of her *feminine wiles* to get what she wanted. And she really wanted this job.

The interview involved a series of standard questions. It also involved a series of questions that she knew was just a ploy to keep her in the room longer. The three men didn't move in their chairs, almost reclining in the leather high-backs, watching every deliberate movement of Ashley's fingers, pushing an imaginary strand of hair from her face, resting ever so lightly on her knee, sliding across her chest, a single finger moving over her lower lip when she seemed to be contemplating a question!

Her eyes didn't move off the middle-aged executives either, all of them varying degrees of handsome, and all of them looking like they worked out. Ashley wouldn't mind having a second, more intimate interview with any of them, she thought, making sure, without saying it, that they knew this.

"Well, thank you for your time, Ashley," Charles said, Rod and Ben, echoing the sentiment. As she got up to leave, only Ben stood up, the other two unable to. Ashley smiled inside, knowing that she had done all she could. Now she had to go into supportive friend mode because Jillian was up next, Charles instructing her to send Jillian in on her way out!

"They're hot," Ashley whispered to Jillian. "Go get 'em!"

"You'll wait for me?" Jillian asked, looking a little too nervous.

"Of course, I will. Now just breathe. You've got this!"

Jillian walked confidently towards the table, hiding the erratic beating of her heart. She had never been to a job interview before in her life, and even though she graduated with better marks than Ashley, Ashley had an interview and work experience, from back in college. Her own folks refused for her to work, not wanting anything to distract Jillian from her studies.

Ashley was right. All three men were hot, which intimidated Jillian just that much more. She knew though that she had less than five seconds to recover if she was going to stand a chance. She took a deep breath, leaned back in her chair, and decided to use what she had to gain an advantage, remembering what Ashley had quoted from the article a while ago in the waiting room.

She decided to focus on Charles since those words were his and she wasn't sure about the others.

"Do you know the woman who was in here before you?" Ben asked suddenly, throwing Jillian slightly halfway through the interview.

"Yes, we've been friends since college," she said, shifting her focus from Charles for a minute.

"I thought so," Ben said, and then left it. Jillian really wanted an explanation, but it soon became obvious that this was not to be forthcoming, the three men having a not-so-private conversation now.

"Is she still here?" Charles asked his eyes on Jillian's legs for the millionth time during this interview. He really seemed fixated.

"She's waiting for me," Jillian said, still unsure where exactly this was going.

"Can we get her back in here, if you don't mind?" They all seemed to really want to see Ashley again, and so Jillian started to thank them, getting up to leave.

"No," Charles said. " We'd like both of you in here, *together*. Again, only if you don't mind!"

Jillian didn't mind, remembering every time she and

Ashley had wanted something and gone after it together. These three men had no idea what they were in for, even though up until this point, they seemed to be in charge. Little did they know that the script was about to be entirely flipped!

CHAPTER 3

"ARE THE TWO OF YOU COMPETITIVE?" Ben asked the first to gather himself. Seeing Jillian and Ashley side by side really was something spectacular.

"A little... But we've found, in the past, that we work much, much better together..." Jillian spoke with new confidence now, feeding off Ashley's energy.

"Is this so?" Ron was looking at Ashley.

"We've gotten ourselves out of a few sticky situations together, yes. Granted, we're also guilty of getting ourselves in trouble, together, too!"

There was a long silence.

"I'm sure I'm not the only one curious to know what kind of trouble?" Charles cut straight to it.

"We could never tell you that," Ashley said, feigning shyness.

"At least not in a job interview..." Jillian added, winking.

"And if this wasn't an interview?" Charles asked no one in particular, his hand under his vest, pulling hard on his nipples. He couldn't hide that these two made him very, very excited.

Jillian and Ashley looked at each other. They knew that all bets were off if this went wrong. They also knew that if they were reading the culture of this agency wrong, they could be blacklisted. Charles's comments in the article might have been a misquote, but given the feeling they had gotten from the minute they walked through the doors of the building, both women seriously doubted it.

They didn't speak to each other, but they had made up their minds to throw caution to the wind, and play their hand. If it went badly, then it did. But at least they would have had lots of fun crashing and burning.

Wild Things was a rogue agency, ahead of its time. Where others saw a workplace that objectified women, Ashley and Jillian, both hardcore feminists, saw a place that celebrated women, allowing them to play by the same rules men had manipulated for centuries. Both of them really wanted to work here. And so, with just a look, and a subtle nod, they agreed to do everything in their power to ensure a position at the agency by the time they left this room.

"Well, if this wasn't an interview..." Ashley said, getting up and locking the door while Jillian tuned over the clipboards in front of the three men who already seemed to be sweating at the suggestion of this whole new take on the *not-an-interview* interview!

"Then we might want to move to the comfort of that *very, very large* sofa by the window," Jillian said, pointing to the rather long four-division leather sofa that ended in a daybed. The cream-colored L-shape really seemed designed for what they had in mind.

What they had in mind had probably played out on this sofa many times, they thought. The pair knew, however, that it had never been played out with them, and so this would, technically speaking, be the sofa's maiden voyage!

The sun kissed the sofa from outside, dancing over the bodies of the two women now unbuttoning their shirts. Then they slowly unzipped their skirts, stepping out of them carefully. Ron and Charles were seated already, Ben sliding over a high-back so that they could put their clothing on it nearly. Appreciating this forethought, Ashley and Jillian stopped him before he could sit. Ashley helped him out of his golf shirt, Jillian making light work of his chinos.

The dream team got on their knees and took turns kissing Ben's quick-to-respond manhood. His underwear was in the way and it wasn't. There was no particular hurry now, what with all the bosses in the room with them. Ashley stretched her mouth over the cotton, sandwiching his sausage between her lips. Jillian kissed the back of his incredible thighs.

Then, as one, they slowly freed him from his briefs. Jillian bit lightly into his bum, Ashley breathing in his man-scent through his pubic hair. All the while their hands moved as far up his chest and back as they would go.

The room was deathly quiet now. Charles and Ron had unzipped their own trousers. Both men rubbed themselves underneath their own underwear, just the tips of their own love muscles exposed. Ron was dripping, using this light flow to coat his dome, using his index. Charles was pulling hard on himself, slowly.

"You lucky dawg," Charles muttered.

"Pays to be a gentleman," Ben whispered, looking down to where both delicious creatures were now nibbling on his jewels. He placed a hand on their heads, looking every bit like a man who'd just been knighted!

Twenty fingers worked in perfect synchronicity on his member, gently touching, gently squeezing, ever so gently pulling. Two tongues moved over the entire surface of his *low hangers.* Ben's eyes bulged out of their sockets as he took short, sharp breaths. He pressed harder on their heads and planted his feet firmly into the rug, gripping the mohair with his toes. He was really struggling to hold on to his center but wanted to do nothing that would bring this dual assault to an end.

The two tongues started working up his length, and when both moved in little circles on his head, his lips quivered. He was trying to speak, but couldn't, planting himself deeper into the rug, scared that he would either fall over, or fly away. Ben grabbed onto their hair now, careful not to pull. He watched as their tongues snaked away from each other, and then came together, them kissing one another without removing their lips off him.

Then they were licking, down towards where his nuts seemed to have dropped an inch. This worked perfectly for this duo because Jillian was able to take both of them into her mouth as Ashley wrapped her perfect mouth around his head and slowly started to hide him inside her face.

Charles and Ron watched closely, a mixture of envy and delight. Their own trousers were now down to their knees, both of them coating their shafts with the steady trickle escaping their throbbing domes. They desperately wanted in on the action now, but to disturb Ben's bliss would've just been rude!

CHAPTER 4

BEN WATCHED as every inch of him vanished, watched as it slowly reappeared. Again, one glorious inch at a time, he disappeared, and no sooner was he all gone when he suddenly reappeared. The lips wrapped around him were perfection. The mouth making this magic possible over and over again, *heaven*.

Jillian was hanging from his thighs, upside down, which stabilized him. She was working every part of her own delicious mouth on his orbs. Ben watched as the pair's enthusiasm for him grew, enjoying the advancing techniques being introduced to him. He'd really never experienced such expert mouths in his life.

"I'm close..." he whispered. Then he said it a little louder, needing to warn especially Ashley.

She used her lips to squeeze the base of his shaft, paused a little, and then slowly freed him from her mouth. Jillian released his balls and stood up. They walked Ben over to the sofa and sat him down. Charlie and Ron had by this time kicked their trousers off completely, their tops discarded too. They watched as Ashley kissed Ben, on his neck, then on his mouth. They watched as Jillian now swallowed him, inch by solid inch.

She brought Ben close, and then stopped, brought him close again, and then removed him completely from her mouth. Ashely was nibbling on his nipples now, Charles and Ron still just limited to observing. And then they just couldn't just watch anymore.

Charles went up to Ashley, removing her bra without disturbing what she was doing. He slowly removed her panties, Ashley writhing out of them without skipping a beat on Ben's chest. Ron did the same to Jillian, who also worked with him to get herself completely naked now, without shifting her mouth's focus from the task at hand.

Jillian was on her knees, working Ben close again with her mouth. Ron parted her legs, and slid underneath her, upside down, so that her pink perfection hung just above his mouth. Taking hold of her thighs, he lifted himself until he connected, kissing ever so gently before sucking incredibly hard, his relief audible.

Then he was licking, the outside of Jillian coated lightly from the inside. She shuddered a moment and then pressed herself hard into his mouth, to which he responded by sucking on her even harder. Suddenly he was inside her with his tongue, Jillian pushing harder still against his mouth.

She was enjoying this as much, if not more, than the man doing it to her.

Charles got behind Ashley and started to kiss the back of her neck. Then his lips moved up and down on her back, softly. His hands moved over her thighs, and then over her belly. Quickly, he found her breasts, pressing down on them gently, moving his hardness against her perfect *tushy*!

He was coating her beautiful skin with the occasional

drippage from himself, using his head to move it around on her, all the while squeezing her breasts, still gently. Ashley's mouth moved from one of Ben's nipples to the other, and then back again. Then she kissed him down his belly, meeting Jillian on Ben's penis. They were now pushing, Ashley against Charles, Jillian just that much harder into Ron's mouth.

Then Charles too was underneath Ashley, mimicking Ron, although he was more comfortable on the sofa than Ron was on the floor. Charles was French kissing her happy place, and Ashley was ecstatic. Although, he wasn't sure, because the sounds she was making seemed directly linked to Ben in her mouth.

The two women worked in tandem on Ben, keeping his orgasm just out of reach. This started to frustrate him, and he held Ashley on him, thrusting into her mouth, needing to shoot just once. But she took his hand off her head, lifted herself off him, and let Jillian take her place. Ben tried the same thing with her too, but no sooner was he thinking he would blow, and her mouth too was gone.

This started to feel more and more like punishment, now. It really wasn't intentional, and the two women might have let him erupt a while ago. But they were caught up in a wonderful circuit, en route to their own orgasms, the men between their legs bringing them both incredibly close now.

Ashley's orgasm rolled over her in a surprising wave. She was off Ben now, arching her back, Charles's tongue deep inside her, extracting the most intense pleasure from her. This pleasure flowed from her, into his mouth, coating his tongue, letting him get that much deeper into her. She let out a few mild screams, not loud, more like protracted exhalations.

Jillian followed just after, Ben in her mouth muffling

the sounds that would have escaped her otherwise. She pressed into Ron's mouth and then pulled away, before pressing back into his mouth hard. He had expertly brought her to a super climax, and she wanted to thank him. Ashley too wanted to thank Charles, but she looked down at Ben, realizing that they still had unfinished business.

Both women licked the sides of his shaft for a minute, but it was Ashley who eventually took it into her mouth, Jillian again finding his nuts. There was something about the way Ashley sucked on him now that let him know that relief was on the way. She did it hard and with purpose, pulling his orgasm from him, it seemed.

What Jillian was managing on his balls was gentle, though. This contrast was initially confusing, and again Ben thought his orgasm would be just out of reach. But then suddenly the two opposing sensations clicked, and his body and mind started their unified trajectory towards the climax.

He erupted hard, not trying at all to muffle his moans. He didn't care who heard him. He couldn't care who heard him. Charles and Ron didn't seem to mind either, probably because this sound and many like it were all too familiar around the office.

"Thank you... Thank you... Thank you..." was all Ben could manage as Ashley swallowed his not too excessive load!

CHAPTER 5

RON POURED HIMSELF A DRINK. It was a little early in the day, but this was his thing. Charles took a bottle of water from the fridge, offering the women something to drink. They both declined.

Ben was now sitting on the daybed part of the sofa, half reclining. He was still in a bit of a haze, his body still expelling fluid in a slow trickle from his now-flaccid tip. He used his fingers to coat his softness with this liquid, desperately wanting to resurrect his erection quickly.

It would take a minute though, so it was he who would now be the spectator!

"You two are very naughty," Charles said, pulling Ashley and Jillian to where he was now sitting on the couch.

"You really have no idea," Jillian said, lying across the seat of the sofa, her head in Charles's lap. She took him into her mouth, enjoying the already steady pre-flow, which was quite excessive. Her mouth worked up and down on him slowly, absolutely no hurry on her part because she was quite comfortable. Charles moved lower on the seat, adjusting himself for maximum comfort.

Ashley was on her knees on the opposite side of him. She was pulling on his nipples, as aggressively as he had been pulling on himself at the table earlier. Charles held her face to his, planting quick kisses on her mouth and the side of her face. She was kissing him too, rubbing her own moist place against his arm until he too was pulling on her lovely lips with the tip of his finger, mimicking what she was doing on his tits.

Ron was standing close, drink in hand. He too was just watching now, his free hand moving on himself. He threw his eyes at Ben and snickered, mocking his colleague's attempt to get hard. Ben threw him a 'mock me now' look, and stood up to get a drink of his own. Then he came and stood next to Ron, put a hand on his shoulder, and then stepped forward to where Ashley and Charles were now French kissing.

"Excuse me," he said, moving Ashley's mouth to his still-softness. She used just her lips to get the sponge into her mouth, not wanting to remove her fingers from the pleasure points drawing moans from Charles. She was also moaning now, as much because of Charles's fingertips, as for the hardening mass in her mouth.

Ben looked at Ron again, his arm around his neck.

"See?!"

Ron downed his drink and put down his glass. He mock-cracked his knuckles and swung out from under Ben's arm. He got on the sofa, lifted Jillian's legs onto his lap, and edged his way in, towards her middle. He was still solid, his shaft grazing her legs as he moved on the sofa, lifting Jillian slightly as he went.

Then he parted her legs a bit, and he too was now

fondling her feminine bits, also with just the tips of his fingers. There seemed to be unspoken competitiveness between him and Ben especially, and he was determined that he would win, knowing what winning would constitute, for him at least.

Ron took some of the fluid from himself, coated his fingertip, and then ever so slowly eased this single finger into Jillian. She pushed down on the finger, guiding it completely into herself. She didn't skip a beat on Charles, though, her mouth moving up and down on him with the same sensual ease with which the single finger was now moving in and out of her.

Ashley moved her mouth from Ben to Charles's nipples, not quite sucking, more biting. He moaned louder, sending a finger up into her fast. Then he added another finger as she bit harder into him. They seemed to be playing a game of *anything you can do*, and Charles was winning. Ashely removed her mouth from him when he had made full entry with the two, finding solace in Ben's firmness.

Ron's eyes were on Charles's fingers, as he too went for two now. He got these double digits all the way inside her too, with relative ease. Moving inside her now in every direction, Ron really wanted another part of him to replace his fingers. He looked at Charles, then at Jillian's entrance. He wondered how much of a disrupting influence he would be, already getting on his knees and positioning himself on top of her.

Charles's eyes were now on him. Ben's too. Both men watched as Ron lifted and pushed, getting Jillian onto her knees. Then they both watched as Ron's hard, thickness slid as easily into her as his fingers had. Ron sucked the flavors of her from his fingers as he made his entry into her completely.

His thrusts were slow and steady. His eyes locked with Ben's, and they nodded at each other, these nods meaning different things to both men. Then Ron's eyes were on where he was playing a very erotic version of *now you see me, now you don't*. He thrust into her and pulled out of her like he had all the time in the world, and also like he thought he had a much longer penis than he actually had!

Jillian's arch was incredible. Charles reached over it, placing a hand firmly on her behind. He pulled toward him, lifting her just that much more, giving himself a better view, and also giving Ron Fuller access. He also wanted to be inside Ashley now, but Ben was already lifting her off his fingers and away from him. He watched as Ben carried her to the board table. Charlie pulled Jillian's mouth off him and fed her the taste of her friend, watching as Ron again went all the way in.

Then he brought her mouth back onto himself, reaching for her perfect cheeks with both hands. He pulled them apart, revealing to Ron an alternative, knowing that he would understand the trade-off he wanted to make now!

CHAPTER 6

RON WAS REALLY STILL ENJOYING his position in Jillian, though. He was looking at Charles and then looked back at himself moving in and out of her, lulled into an almost dream. She felt as good as the whole scene looked, and Ron knew that if Charles could see things from his vantage point, he wouldn't be suggesting what he was.

It was clear to Charles that this wasn't going to happen yet. He looked over to where Ben and Ashley had just gotten to the table. They looked like they were still figuring things out, so Charles knew he couldn't interrupt. He pulled Jillian's mouth off him, kissed her, and then put her back on himself, knowing that for the moment at least, this was as good as it was going to get.

Charles came close a few times, each time lifting Jillian away from him. He knew himself, and he knew that he probably had one good orgasm in him. He was throbbing now, wanting to blow. But he wanted to blow inside one of the beautiful women in the conference room, an orgasm too beautiful a thing to waste on a mouth.

If he had the whole day, or a whole night, he would

have risked it. He couldn't, now, he knew, so he would wait. He just hoped he wouldn't have to wait too long.

Ron had both hands on Jillian's hips now, moving her back and forth on himself. He was not moving at all. Charles held her head, moving her up and down on himself, leaving her behind alone now, hoping that limiting his involvement would speed things up.

"Damn, this is good..." Ron said, pulling her all the way onto what was really a perfectly average penis. It was thick, but only just. And he didn't really have too much length. But again, he was moving in and out of Jillian like he thought he had much more.

"You don't say," Charles said, lifting Jillian off him for the millionth time. He was dangerously close again.

Frustrated, he maneuvered away from Jillian and went to get himself a drink stronger than water. He didn't touch himself at all, even though this is what he really wanted to do. Instead, he looked over at Ben and Ashley, promising himself in his head that soon enough he would have access to a body. From what he was seeing on the boardroom table, he suddenly hoped that this would be Ashley's.

Ben was on his back on the table, Ashley on top of him. She was moving like she had a point to prove, and she was going to take her time proving it. Her entire lower body pulled Ben's erection in every direction, each movement meticulous. Her hands pulled on her own breasts, and the whole performance looked like a show she was putting on exclusively for Ben's benefit.

Charles walked over to the table, drink in hand. He watched the performance a while and then started to run his fingers up and down Ashley, on her back, and on her front. She moved her hands, giving him access to her breasts, which he squeezed gently. He leaned over the table and kissed her on her mouth, playing with the outside of her while Ben still snuggly occupied the inside.

Ashley moved harder on Ben, harder against the fingers manipulating her lips. She grabbed Charles's head, almost pulling him up onto the table. The multiple sensations playing out on her obviously drove her wild. And wild was obviously something she liked very very much.

"Inside," she whispered.

"What?" Charles asked, not sure what she was saying.

"In...Side..." She was louder now, pushing his hand against her as Ben was being moved around and around inside. Charles thought he knew what she meant now, and he looked down to where her body met Ben's. Slowly slowly, against Ben's thicker penis, he started to press his index finger into her. Her body gave way, but it was still an incredibly tight fit.

Charles didn't mind that his own hand was making direct contact with Ben's erection. This had nothing to do with that, and everything to do with pleasing Ashley, who was eager to please them too, she had proven. Ben didn't mind either, watching as Charles's thick finger joined him inside her. He seemed excited by this, grabbing her waist and pushing her back so that he had a better view, and also so that Charles could work this finger inside her deeper.

Charles got in all the way too. Then he moved his finger to the rhythm of Ashley's other occupant. She was wet now, really wet, and he moved in her with an ease that made him wonder if it was possible for him to add another. He knew he had thick fingers. He knew he had long fingers. And when he pulled his index out of her, he knew that he had a finger that Ashley really wanted inside his.

He gave her his finger to lick. She did so, slowly. And then he was inside her again, firstly with just his index again, and then his index and middle. Again the fit was tight, and the entry was not easy. But she really wanted it and he wanted it and Ben wanted it and so they all worked together to make this possible.

Ben was caught between wanting to erupt now, and enjoying what he was seeing. So he paced himself, held himself back, keeping himself on the edge but not going over it. Again Charles was frustrated, knowing that he was partly, if not mostly, to blame for this new delay. His fingers were not his anymore, either, Ashley using every muscle in herself to keep full control of *everything* inside her.

Charles was enjoying the show. He enjoyed his part in it. But he needed to experience the thrill of a woman soon or he really was going to lose his mind. He knew that Ben or Ron could have given him a chance, easily, both of them with a lot more staying power than he. He thought of pulling rank, regaining control of this interview. But then he saw Jillian walking towards him, and knew the wouldn't have to.

CHAPTER 7

JILLIAN GOT onto the table and lay on her back. She moved a single finger into herself, her knees bent, her feet flat on the table. She was lying next to Ben actually, and he turned his face so that he and Jillian were now kissing. Charles slowly removed his fingers from Ashley and went to attend to the woman who had saved this situation from imploding.

Jillian had actually saved Charles from imploding.

Charles slid her down the glass, towards himself. He pushed her legs up so that she was hanging over him. Thankfully Charles had the *length* to make this position work for both him and Jillian.

He exhaled loudly as he went into her. Charles made full entry, his upper thighs against the side of the table. Jillian rested her legs on his chest, her knees bent over his shoulders. Charles bent forward a bit to make this possible.

He wasn't thrusting yet. There was no need to, every part of Jillian's *juicy deliciousness* moving over his shaft. It was a magnificent squeeze, every muscle seeming to move over every inch of Charles. He looked at where he couldn't see himself, almost *seeing* what was happening to him.

"How are you doing that," he asked.

"It's a little early to let you in on *all* my secrets..." she replied, looking also where they were connected.

"Then I suppose I should just enjoy being *in* you," Charles said, positioning her closer to him as he started to drive himself into her.

The urgency that threatened to overwhelm him had dissipated completely now. He knew, for the first time really, why it was that Ron had difficulty letting go of his position on Jillian, his position in her. Her body seemed to work in independent pockets, each one capable of executing epic servings of erotic excellence. He held her in place, moving himself all the way into her and then out, enjoying each and every stroke!

Charles too had incredibly powerful legs, it seemed because he was standing solid, the movement driven essentially by his own internal engine. It was in fact his powerful gluts driving him, and he himself was incredibly glad that he never ever skipped leg day at the gym. For his age, his body worked remarkably well, and even though he was usually spent after a single orgasm, one orgasm was all he usually needed.

Jillian too enjoyed the fullness of his entry. He had the technique, and the tools, to deliver. And as he *delivered* himself over and over into her, he brought her to the edge of ecstasy, pulling her just that much more off the edge of the table. Her sweat on her back made movement on the glass uncomfortable, and while Charles couldn't feel it, he could see it. He reached down and lifted her off the table, maintaining their pleasure connection.

Charles managed quite easily to get them back to the

sofa. He put Jillian down, bringing himself down on top of her. He settled himself deeper in her and brought down his full weight on her. Jillian moaned, and then she was quiet. Each time Charles went in, she moaned again, silent on the exit.

"You're incredible..." he said.

"That she is," Ron said, looking like he wanted to be back inside her.

Charles was the one playing Monopoly now, not prepared to move. He just fed himself over and over to her, his forehead pressed hard against her shoulder. He didn't look at Ron, making it obvious that he was not prepared to move.

Ron rubbed his erection, almost apologetically. He was trickling his usual trickle, coating himself with this flow. He squeezed himself a little harder and pulled on himself harder still. He moved closer to Charles, who sensed his approach and held on to Jillian tighter, going in deeper.

His thrusting wasn't vigorous. It was measured, deliciously slow. He used every part of him on every part of her, unable to think of anything else right now. He was in a trance of his own now, present, but not quite there. He felt every part of her, his head going to heaven and coming back with each and every movement.

Ron got to the table just as Ben finished in Ashley. He sat red-faced on the edge of the table, looking like he needed a drink. Ron gave him his, and then pressed himself against Ashley, pushing her against the side of the table. She pressed herself against him too, grinding into him so that they moved against each other with no penetration.

She bit into his nipples as Ben watched. She lifted herself up back onto the table and wrapped her legs around Ron, pulling him closer still. He might not have had full comprehension of his size, but she certainly did. And not being one to engage in lackluster intimacy just for the sake of, needing to enjoy it too, she thought of how best to utilize Ron's average hard-on.

Ashley pushed herself off the table, pushing Ron backward as she did. She turned to face the table, leaning over the shiny, sweaty surface. Planting her feet firmly into the floor, she parted her legs, hanging every desired part of her over the table. Ron came up behind her, and moved closer. He was suddenly unsure which of the beautiful options he would take.

He remembered Jillian's beautiful rear, exposed when Charles had pulled her cheeks apart. He knew that Ashley's would be as beautiful, separating her cheeks to get a look for himself. When he exposed the succulent, inviting hole, he knew that the decision had been made.

"Do you mind," he asked as he rubbed his head against this inviting place.

"Mind?" she asked, raising her behind higher, pushing it against Ron's rod, which threatened entry even before she could answer.

Ron took a hold of her hips, using the fingers of the other hand to keep himself pointed at a downward angle so that he could make quick work of this entry. Her body received him, easily, and Ron soon held both her hips, pushing her back and forth as he took a hold of this almost sacred hole.

CHAPTER 8

BEN TOOK A CALL, and sat, drink in hand, on the opposite end of the sofa. He watched Charles move in Jillian, excited again but not hard. He held himself with his free hand, holding the phone with the other one. His glass slid against his softness, sending an interesting sensation into him.

For as long as he was on the phone, he didn't take his eyes off of Jillian, who was further up on the daybed, looking at him too. The look on her face said that she was enthralled by the man in her, a man who was surprising himself with how long he was lasting. The enjoyment was definitely mutual.

Ron was making a hell of a lot of noise now. Ben didn't need to look at him to know why. Ashley was enjoying Ron in her too, although she wasn't making nearly as much noise. Her head rested comfortably on her arms as he thrust in and out of her, all the excitement of a bull in a china shop!

Jillian's legs were wrapped around Charles now. She had had two, maybe three mild orgasms, Charles still working his way up to one. His movement now, singular in purpose, let her know that it wouldn't be long. She used her body to will him over to the *Promised Land*.

But then Charles slid himself out of her completely. Her body shook at this rapid and unexpected exit. He lifted himself off her, and even though he looked like this was the last thing he wanted to be doing, he kissed her on her forehead and left her on the sofa wondering what just happened.

She touched herself and went into herself with two fingers. She was incredibly wet. The memories of the mild orgasms she just had lingered in her head, like a dream. She wasn't sure they had happened, but her body told her the whole story.

She watched Charles go over to where Ron was still occupying Ashley from the back, in her back. He watched as the big boss whispered something in Ron's ear that saw him make an agonizing extraction. Then the three of them were walking toward the sofa, and both she and Ben watched the trio approach.

Ben moved closer to Jillian, to allow the three bodies space on the sofa. He watched, as did Jillian, as Charles lay down on his back first. Then they watched Ashley mount him, before Ron resumed his place, lying almost on top of her now, Ashley lying on top of Charles.

This sandwich worked on every level. It gave Charles full access to Ashley while eliminating the need for him to do any work. It was time now, for him, and he just wanted to relax into it and, in essence, be brought to an end with minimal participation. He wasn't a lazy lover by any extension of the imagination. He had just proven this with Jillian.

But he did know what he liked, knew what he wanted, and was accustomed to always getting exactly that!

Ron's size didn't matter in this new position either,

which worked exceptionally well for him. It made his length irrelevant because he was powered now by his whole body. He thought he'd had full access to her before, but only now, when Ashley lifted herself slightly off Charles, and into him, did he really know what full access was.

Jillian and Ben watched this tantalizing moment, watched these two middle-aged men share Ashley rather equally. They couldn't see her face, couldn't see any of their faces, but now Ashley was making all the right noises. She had a spot. She had several. And all these spots were now being unequivocally *hit*!

There really was no particular need for engagement sexually, by the spectators. Ben lay close to Jillian, running his fingers up and down the length of her, with no intention in particular. She touched him, casually, almost carelessly, with no intention on her part either. Ben was hard then he was not. Then he sported a perfectly acceptable semi, but still, neither of them thought this had to mean anything.

"As far as interviews go,' Ben started.

"As far as interviews go?" Jillian asked, looking at him with just a glimmer of the cheek.

"Right, right... This wasn't an interview!"

Ben brought his mouth to Jillian's, connected. They kissed long, deep, with the passionate familiarity of lovers. They might have been. If the meeting was under different circumstances, they actually could have been, Jillian thought.

"It was interesting," Jillian said when she moved away to breathe.

"Just *interesting*," Ben said, seeming genuinely offended.

"Let's just say that it could be a whole lot better than interesting if we worked here!" Jillian couldn't resist the opportunity. This was, despite what anybody said, an actual interview. The dynamics of the process might have been different, but there was a job to be had, and both Jillian and Ashley wanted this job. This was, after all, what had brought them to *Wild Things* in the first place.

Ashley was making real noise now. The sounds coming from her were no longer subdued. She was making no effort to be quiet. She couldn't. Charles had gripped her tightly and held her against himself as he almost breathed his orgasm violently into her. He was pinned to the sofa, but he shook so wildly that Ron almost lost his hold.

Just almost!

Ashley was still caught in the throws of her own orgasm as Ron regained momentum. He was terribly close before the earthquake. But then he wasn't. Now, though, he had regained rhythm, and he could see the other side, across the *Jordan*. It looked beautiful, and he was in no hurry to cross, even though the inevitability of this crossing was becoming more and more apparent.

He managed to hold off for a dozen perfectly executed thrusts. And then, after what really was an eternity of ecstasy, he too was done!

CHAPTER 9

GETTING Ashley off Charles was an exercise requiring thought and careful precision. He couldn't move, and Ron didn't want to. Both men were still incredibly hard, much to both their surprise and delight. Ashley made small involuntary movements into both men, both still throbbing inside her.

The biggest surprise was Ron. His penis seemed to take on a life of its own, breathing almost. It huffed and puffed, expanded and contracted. It felt incredibly hot inside her too, lulling her tender hole into willing submission. She too didn't want him to move, even as Charles started to mumbled something about his circulation.

Ashley gripped Ron in place as she edged upwards on Charles. This took a long time, but then he popped out of her, still rock solid. She pressed down on his chest as gently as she could and then pressed against Ron in one fluid motion that brought her to her knees. Ron too was on his knees, stilled locked firmly in place.

Charles rolled off the sofa and lay on the floor. He was looking at Ashley, appreciation written all over his face.

Unable to move, he just lay there and stared at the ceiling. Ashley smiled, knowing that he was now completely aware of her power. She hoped, secretly, that it would be enough.

Ron was still breathing inside her. She leaned forward, lifted herself into him just that much more, and relaxed into whatever it was that Ron still wanted to do to her. It seemed to be nothing, though. He seemed too content with their current situation. So content that, for the longest time, he didn't even move.

And then he was moving again. He had no intention of finishing, but the inside of Ashley felt like a place he didn't want to leave. She wasn't moving, still, though, but she was definitely with him. Ron pumped into her steadily, each stroke long and protracted. Ashley was just moaning softly now, the sweat running down her forehead the only sign of her recent exertion.

Ben and Jillian were still not quite touching each other. Yes, their hands were on one another, moving, feeling, fondling, fiddling. But they weren't exactly touching, at least not in any way that looked like it would lead anywhere.

They weren't even looking at each other, not really. Their attention was still on Ron and Ashley, and what they weren't exactly doing. They weren't exactly making love, but their bodies were connected in places that made it seem like they were. If they wanted to, they could have been. But the way things were right now was just perfect.

Ashley knew that she had another orgasm in her. She had several actually. But she knew that Charles was in no position to deliver, and she didn't want to put the kind of pressure on Ron that would see him soft and out of her. It was a strange sort of stalemate, and the queen was not about to make any sort of major moves.

She looked back for the first time to where Jillian and Ben lay. They seemed haphazard about what they were doing to each other, even though Ben was now rock hard. Ashley wanted to call him over to her, but she had no idea how long or how hard Jillian had worked to get him as aroused as he was. Also, she knew that she had had him already, and Jillian might want a go, given that she was the reason for his current erection.

Risking it, she started to move slowly on Ron. Ron responded by moving back, so that what they were doing resembled lovemaking just that much more. Ashely leaned forward just a little too much and he was out of her. Quickly he came down on her and entered her with equal speed.

Jillian was inspired now, and she hung herself over Ben's face and took him into her mouth. She dropped into his mouth, as she worked him in and then out of hers. This day had gone perfectly to script, as far as unscripted encounters went, and because she wasn't sure how it would all end, she needed to at least have one more go on the merry-go-round before she left.

She looked at Charles, still on the floor, looking at them and not. He looked like he couldn't move now even if he wanted to, and this disappointed her just a little because she wanted the same experience Ashley just had. She made a mental note that if she indeed got the job, she would be sure to make this happen, as soon after her appointment as possible.

Ben was inside her with his tongue now, and she wanted him in her with other parts of him. After a short while, she lifted herself out of his mouth and spun around so that they were now face to face. She brought herself down on him, guided him into herself with her own hand, and started to move in delightful circles on him.

She held him tightly around his neck and moved up and down on him before she was again moving around and around. This is not what she wanted, looking over to Ashley, hearing as much as seeing the incredible fun she was having. Jillian now ached in her other place, but she just didn't know how to ask.

She moved up and down on Ben just a moment longer and then lifted herself off him. He looked at her, questioning. Then she turned away from him and lay down on her stomach. With her own hands, she separated her curvaceous cheeks and lifted them slightly, showing him where she wanted him to go. Ben shook his head in disbelief, throwing his eyes quickly to Ashley and Ron.

"The two of you really work exceptionally well together," he moaned, positioning himself on top of her, guiding himself into her slowly, needing to pace himself because a)he was a little thick, and b)she was deliciously tight.

Jillian sighed relieved, and brought herself flat on the sofa now, as Ben made a full and definite entry!

CHAPTER 10

BEN WAS THRILLED with this alternative space, and Jillian was equally thrilled with his occupancy. She held her cheeks apart a moment longer, as Ben settled completely inside her. Then she too rested her head on her arms, raising herself just a little to facilitate full entry.

She wanted to move too, but couldn't. He really was incredibly thick, and so she had to just let him do what he needed to. She let her middle drop to the sofa now, and Ben came down with his full weight onto her, needing to use all of him to break through her resistance.

She really wasn't resisting him. She just needed a minute to acclimatize herself to his size. It was definitely a case of biting off more than you could chew, and so Jillian needed to be still while Ben stretched her open with great care. He had to also be, and he was, incredibly patient!

Ashley moaned again, louder, Ron having finally eased himself out of her rear and swiftly slid into her front. The entry wasn't complete but it didn't need to be. His determined thrusts more than sufficiently made up for the shortfall. They came to a sweaty, almost too eager end together, and Ron rested on her and in her comfortably. He didn't need to move too because the full weight of him on her was perfectly bearable.

Ben was still struggling. He knew how he wanted to move in Jillian, but the lack of lubrication made this a bit difficult. He eased himself slowly all the way in, settled a bit, and then pulled himself just almost all the way out. At an agonizing pace, he went fully in again, before slowly going partially out. He started to wonder about her comfort and went to her ear to ask her.

Before he could though, she moved so that he was completely out of her. She slid out underneath him and turned onto her back. Then she took him into her softer center and wrapped her legs around him. Out of sheer relief, he thrust into her hard and fast. He filled this canal easily and completely, and soon she was ready for him to try again in the place she really wanted him to be.

Ben gripped her legs and lifted them. He found this oh-so-willing crevice and positioned himself to strike. He went in, slowly but easier in this new position. He pulled her onto him and settled fully in her. A few sensuous thrusts and she let him have her, her body relenting in that beautiful way that bodies do. He was home, now, and he sent her swiftly on towards a massive home run, even though it really was her own fingers that made the final strikes with home base.

When they had finished, all of them, and once they had sufficiently recovered, Ashley and Jillian got dressed. They did so in silence, but this silence was not awkward. All five people in the conference room were exhausted, and they clearly had to reconcile for themselves what this whole process meant.

For the men, it was a successful interview. They really

never expected sex from all their interviewees, but when it happened, it had to be good. This was more than good. This bordered on epic. None of them said as much, though.

Ashley and Jillian caught each other's eyes as they finished getting dressed. Then, again in almost solemn silence, they helped each other with their hair. Then they turned to the men who were now all pulling up their zips at the same time!

Charles put a finger to his lips before they could speak. The three men sat on the sofa now and just gawked at them for the longest time. Now the silence threatened to become uncomfortable.

Ben started to speak, and then stopped himself. He really was stuttering. Charles didn't even try to speak yet, and when Ron tried to salvage the situation, he also couldn't quite speak. They just relaxed into the plush leather and continued to stare.

Ashley and Jillian were also staring, at each other though. They really had no idea what was going on now.

"This has nothing to do with what just happened here," Charles said, at last, "but you start Monday... *Both of you!*"

Ashley and Jillian walked out composed, until they hit the streets, Ashley suddenly letting out an exhilarated scream. Jillian high-fived her, already on the phone to let her folks know that she had got the job!

ABOUT THE AUTHOR

Tena Seldan is an emerging erotica author of many erotica kinks and sub-genres. Be sure to check out other books and leave a review if this story got you hot!

Visit my blog at Tena Seldan Blog
Join my newsletter for exclusive previews
Tena Seldan Newsletter

Sign up for Free Stories from Xplicit Press Authors
Xplicit Press Author Updates
Like Xplicit Press on Facebook
Follow Xplicit Press on Twitter

Readers: I want to expand a few of the stories to see where the characters can be explored further. If there are any of the stories that you would like to read more about again, I'd love to hear from you!

Keep In Touch
Tena Seldan
info@tenaseldan.com